What Will You Be for Halloween?

Mark Todd

Houghton Mifflin Company
Boston 2001

The illustrations are acrylics on paper.

Library of Congress Cataloging-in-Publication Data
Todd, Mark, 1970—
What will you be for Halloween? / Mark Todd.
p.   cm.
Summary: Rhyming text describes a variety of Halloween costumes and characters,
from venomous vampire and hairy werewolf to mysterious mummy and warty witch.
ISBN 0-618-08803-2
[1. Costume—Fiction. 2. Halloween—Fiction. 3. Monsters—Fiction.
4. Stories in rhyme.] I. Title.
PZ8.3.T562 Wh 2001
[E]—dc21
00-033465

Printed in Singapore
TWP 10 9 8 7 6 5 4 3 2 1

FOR LITTLE

LILI

What will you be for Halloween?

A venomous vampire
in a cloak of black.
Sharp teeth,
widow's peak,
hold the garlic, please.

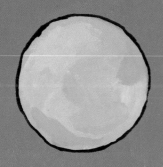

A hairy werewolf
to be wary of.
Howling, snarling, drooling,
with claws and paws,
elongated schnoz.

A mad scientist's monster
with shoulders hunched.
Big and bulky
and often sulky,
a mean, green, sleepwalking machine.

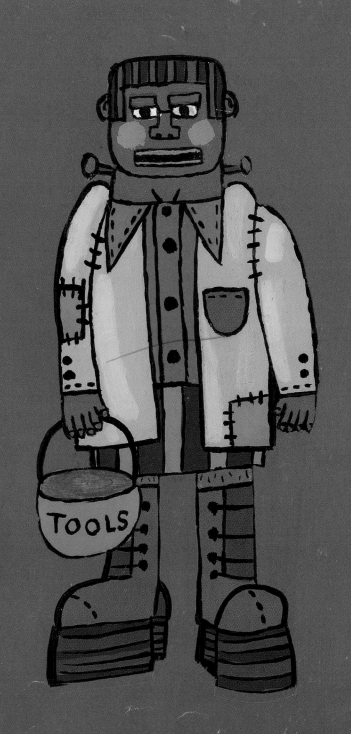

A ghastly ghost,
white and creepy,
mysterious and sneaky.
Actually, there's not much to it—
you can see right through it.

A plundering pirate
in buckles and boots,
eye patch and hook for that genuine look.
Sailing the high seas
for jewels and gems and whatever she sees.

A riveted robot
with circuits and blips and computer chips.
"0-1-1-0-1-0-1"
is "TRICK OR TREAT" in computer lingo,
in case you didn't know.

A scary skeleton,
femurs, funnybones, and ribs.
Thin and shaky,
frail and lanky,
a frightful sight in black and white.

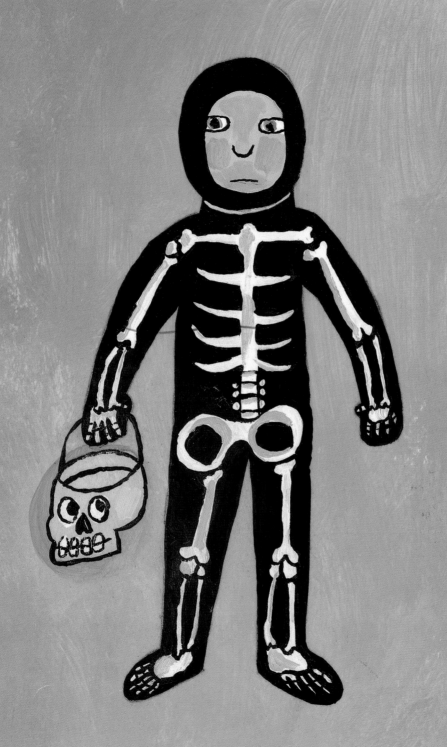

A menacing Martian
with green, googly-eyed antennae.
A strange, shiny space invader,
who beamed down to say hello
from his meteor-powered UFO.

A courageous cowgirl
in spurs and chaps
and a ten-gallon hat.
This outlaw can rope a snack
in three seconds flat.

A mysterious mummy,
groaning and moaning,
bandaged from head to toe.
What he really looks like,
only his mummy knows.

A warty witch
with broom and pointed hat.
Curly toes, striped hose,
all in black—
even her cat.

Now that you have chosen what you will be,
it's time to go.
It's time to meet
all the others and . . .